Henry Peterson

Faire-Mount

Henry Peterson

Faire-Mount

ISBN/EAN: 9783337317195

Printed in Europe, USA, Canada, Australia, Japan

Cover: Foto ©Andreas Hilbeck / pixelio.de

More available books at **www.hansebooks.com**

BY

HENRY PETERSON,

AUTHOR OF "PEMBERTON; OR, ONE HUNDRED YEARS AGO," ETC.

PHILADELPHIA:

CLAXTON, REMSEN & HAFFELFINGER,

624, 626 & 628 MARKET STREET.

1874.

COLLINS, PRINTER,
705 JAYNE ST.

List of Illustrations.

v

FAIRE-MOUNT.

O N Schuylkill's banks, where hills of beauty rise,
　　'Neath the deep blue of Pennsylvania's skies,
Where winds the river, 'mid its woods of calm,
Grand and majestic — an embodied psalm —
Where opening vistas, as you onward stray,
New splendors bring to glorify the way,
In the glad days when life and hope were young,
And in the soul their songs tumultuous sung,
Oft have I wandered, from the world apart,
To feed the immortal hunger of the heart.

Precious is Beauty! In this world where care

Lays on us loads that seem too hard to bear,

Where cold and hunger our existence bound

With daily duties, a prosaic round,

And oft, oppressed with grief, we sadly stray,

With leaden heart, beneath a sky of gray,

Without the charm that Beauty's hand has given,

The green-spread landscape, and blue-vaulted heaven,

The clouds fantastic, or aflame with light,

The sunbow's glory, the star-studded night,

Torrents, wild dashing as they downward pour,

The rush of waves upon the rock-bound shore,

Rich curves of woodland, with their leafy bowers,

The sweet and subtle influence of the flowers,

And all the graceful forms and glowing dyes

That Art has mimicked from the earth and skies,

Oh what were Life? what all the dull, dark days

Which even now afflict our devious ways?

A cold, bleak scene — blank, desolate and bare —

Our life a mere existence of despair.

Sacred is Beauty — let us guard it well.

Not idly did the wise Athenian tell

That Beauty was of Virtue but the flower.

No good exists but Beauty is its dower.

And when this globe was made God called it good.

And still 't is beautiful, still therefore good.

And who could doubt it, gazing on this wood

Of solemn Pines, with each its ancient crown —

A natural Temple, cool and dark and brown,—

Or on this wide expanse of wave and hill,

Where birds are singing, and all else is still,

Save the gay laugh of children, or some grand

Burst of far music from the People's band.

Well was it done then — well, and worthy praise —

To consecrate this spot for future days ;

Safe from all greed of Mammon, safe from Pride,

To consecrate it as the city's Bride,

Fair and without a blemish, pure and sweet,

A nursing-mother for our children meet ;

To teach them all that Beauty e'er has taught,

The power of gentleness, the calm of thought,

High breeding from its Poplars straight and tall,

Grand manners from its Oaks — and what we call

The ripest fruit of wisdom, power to own

The right of each to be himself alone —

As says the grass I too my beauty have,

Although my greenness be not of the wave,

And walnut-trees no glance of scorning wear

Because the oaks but worthless acorns bear,

And poplars tulips in their spicy pride,

Each having something to the rest denied,

And each its place in this fair world of ours,

Among the herbs or trees or fruits or flowers.

Yes, these the lessons that the city's Bride

May teach alike to child of toil and pride.

Here may our sons be also taught to prize

The Civic virtues, dear to patriots' eyes.

Be taught that Wealth to mortals is not given,

But simply lent on usury by heaven ;

Not to be squandered with a reckless hand,

But with wise foresight used to bless the land.

And, standing on this Hill, where rolls away,

From slopes of green to distant skies of gray,

A varied scene, where nature blends with art

To please the eye, and elevate the heart,

Where the great city lies outstretched and still,

With naught to tell of all its good and ill,

Save where dun clouds reveal its hidden fires,

Save where devotion upward soars in spires,—

Here may we point our moral, tell of one

Who lived for others, not for self alone;

Bid them forget the man whose only claim

Is that he gave fair cities to the flame,

The famous conqueror, the mighty king,

Who swept the world as on a vulture's wing,

Glutting with human hearts his greedy gorge;—

But bid them reverence the name of GEORGE!*

* Jesse George, who in conjunction with his sister, gave a very valuable
tract of land, including "George's Hill," to the Park.

And bid them too, to love their mother land

With patriotic fire, and from the hand

Of him who would despoil her pluck the spear.

Such lessons fitly may be taught them here.

For to these "Hills" grand ROBERT MORRIS came,

When, a dim light, flashed Freedom's flickering flame,

"THE HILLS"—THE RESIDENCE OF ROBERT MORRIS.

To gain fresh strength from Nature, nerve his heart,

That he might still perform his mighty part,

And bid the struggling Cause, though faith grew cold,

Faint not for want of iron, lead and gold.

2

Of those sad days it was the saddest far —

Our army lay along the Delaware,

Striving to stay Cornwallis' onward march,

And hold secure the keystone of the Arch.

Despondency on every forehead hung,

And sad forebodings fell from every tongue.

"Where shall we go, if driven back once more?"

"To Susquehanna, broad Potomac's shore,

The Alleghany's ridge, the forest sea,

The far Ohio — anywhere, so free!"

So spoke their Chief, the noblest man of men,

And never nobler in all eyes than then.

"I count the fight though, won, until 't is lost;

As yet our foes may find, and to their cost.

Once broke the meshes of the hunter's net,

We all shall have a Merry Christmas yet."

He spoke the word, once more they sallied forth,

Through the cold twilight of the wintry North.

O'er the half-frozen river, like dim ghosts,

Lurid and deadly, sped the patriot hosts;

Loud roared the winds of night, the sleety hail

Smote in their faces, set and stern and pale;

Tracking the frozen ridges with their blood,

They rushed on Trenton, swept it like a flood,

And turned the tide of war.

Not many days,

And stout Cornwallis, wakening, startled says,

"That sounds like thunder!"   Thunder it is, O peer!

It is the patriot army in thy rear,

Safe from thy leaguer, and their country saved!

MORRIS! thy form no reckless bullets braved,

In the red eye of war no eye of thine

Gazed like the planet Mars with steady shine,

Thy hand no sabre held with fateful sway,

Yet was thine too, the triumph of that day!

And here, when all the weary strife was o'er,

Came our great CHIEFTAIN — Chieftain still, and more —

Sad from those cares of State he little loved,

From angry factions by his voice reproved,

From bitter quarrels, painful to his heart,

Where all were right, and all were wrong in part,

To thy calm shades, Belmont, where hemlocks rise

In solemn grandeur to the untroubled skies,

To gaze upon thy landscape fair and wide,

And seek that peace from nature man denied.

Had these old trees a voice, these groves elate

Doubtless could tell a tale of olden state —

Of a cream-colored chariot, gilded bright,

With rosy cupids on its panels dight,

BELMONT IN THE OLDEN TIME.

With crested harness, and six blooded bays,

Dashing at speed along these winding ways, —

Coachman and footmen, gay postilions too,

In white and crimson liveries, span and new,

Flashing and fine, a brilliant cavalcade,

Brightening the sun, and lighting up the shade.

Stops at a quick command the gallant show,

Down spring the obsequious footmen, bowing low,

Out from the chariot steps upon the sward,

Clad in black velvet, at his side a sword,

A tall and stately figure.   Such the tale

These groves might tell unto the listening vale.

And fiery HAMILTON upon this shore,

When war's wild bugle called to strife no more,

Strayed, deeply musing, while his classic head

Bent with its burden sad of anxious dread,

Lest all that had been won were won in vain,

And strife and chaos follow war and pain.

Right arm of him who born was to command,

Eloquent tongue, and penman's ready hand,

Friend of our Chieftain, whether in the field

To bare the sword and interpose the shield,

Or in the hour of peace to build the State,

And make it Free, and also keep it Great,

Thine be the praise with his that still we bear,

No lustre lost, our Country's banner fair.

Thou gav'st the fabric iron strength to meet

The strife of faction, clamor of the street,

The foreign peril — even to withstand

The reckless fury of a brother's hand.

And JEFFERSON perchance, with thoughtful mien,

Strayed from his neighboring home to view the scene;

Gazing with calm and philosophic eye

From this then noisy stream to placid sky,

Noting each herb and grass and tree and flower,

And making useful thus each passing hour,

Practical, pleasant, genial, wise and good,

A friend to all, by all not understood.

His fame is world-wide, for his thoughts have flown

From cold Siberia to the Indian zone —

Wherever man has rights to be maintained,

Wherever Freedom's to be lost or gained,

His words immortal stir that raging sea,

"All are born Equal; all created Free!"

Ah Freedom, word of potent power for good,

So often used, so little understood,

Far more thou meanest than the vulgar thought

That what the people will to do, they ought.

Thy sage of Monticello claimed for each,

Freedom of thought, of action, and of speech,

To worship God as seemed to him most blest,

To live his life as seemed to him the best,

Granting to others all the rights he claimed,

Never of honest word or deed ashamed,

Conscience his rule and holy men his guide,

Prouder of simple Truth than aught beside,

Free from the People's as the Tyrant's rod,

Responsible alone unto his God!

Great truths are many sided, like the spheres —

You cannot bound them with your narrow fears;

And every Truth is of all Truth a part —

Yet, "What is Truth?" cries Pilate in the heart.

Greatest of questions! He that answer gives,

Even in part, as an Immortal lives.

And often here, beneath the summer's sun,

Our Newton and our Socrates in one,

Came to refresh his soul by Schuylkill's side,

And wander through these wood-paths far and wide.

Dear to his heart, as dear as native earth,

The soil which gave him friends and wife and hearth.

These were the scenes he loved, and this the sky

On which he bent his calm and thoughtful eye ; —

That thunder-cloud, which rears its threatening form,

Dread parent of the lightning and the storm,

Is kin to that with which his spirit strove,

And wrested from its grasp the bolts of Jove,

While on its lurid arch with pen of flame

The vanquished lightning wrote a FRANKLIN'S name.

Oh could the sage and patriot but return

From heights celestial to this earthly bourne,

What keen delight his philanthropic mind

In all the wonders of our age would find —

The marvellous ship, that scorns both wind and tide,

The iron steed a thousand men might ride,

The magic wire, from his own kite-string planned,

Through which, though seas divide, land speaks to land.

At sight of these, would he not backward start,

With a bewildered gaze and throbbing heart? —

Vain thought! and fit to move an angel's mirth.

Can we think heaven a lesser place than earth?

Or that a FRANKLIN, in that grander sphere,

Lingers behind the march of Science here?

And hither came the BARD who struck the lyre

Of Love and Erin with a hand of fire,

And bade in Tara's hall resound once more

The soul of music as in days of yore.

MOORE'S COTTAGE.

"I knew by the smoke that so gracefully curled
    Above the green elms, that a cottage was near;
And I said, 'if there's peace to be found in this world,
    A heart that is humble might hope for it here.'"

A wanderer on Schuylkill's banks he roved,

Far from the friends and scenes he dearly loved,

Till his full soul forgot its wish to roam,

And rested here as in a dream of home.

Still stands the cottage, tottering now and bent,

Where once the poet sang in sweet content,

And thought if Peace e'er dwelt in earthly sphere,

The humble heart might hope to find it here.

Pause we a moment and behold the scene —

Earth has no fairer.   Mid its hills of green,

Where play the sunbeams with the shadows dun,

A mighty mirror shining in the sun,

Lies the broad river, while on either hand

Stretch graceful arches, joining land to land.

Above the wood, a massive pile of white,

In classic grandeur, ravishing the sight,

Thy generous gift, GIRARD, gleams proud and high,

Outlined against the dim and distant sky.

A mass of red the outstretched city glows,

A line of white the distant river flows,

And all around are wooded hill and glade,

And graceful curves, and play of light and shade,

While o'er the heated brow and troubled mind

Flow the cool waves of the rejoicing wind.

Oh who can gaze on such a scene nor feel

What pen can ne'er express, nor words reveal —

Some thought as if within a fairer clime

We once had dwelt in happiness sublime!

These are perchance but stirrings of the wings

On which we yet shall soar to higher things,

When all these earthly bonds shall broken lie,

And the freed spirit seek its native sky.

VIEW FROM BELMONT.

But pass we on where Wissahickon's flood,

Mid the dark stretches of primeval wood,

Where swings the grape, and wild the laurel grows,

By rocky steep and darksome defile flows,

Through many a deep ravine and shadowy glen,

As if a thousand miles from haunts of men.

Here dwelt young KELPIUS with his chosen band,

Exiles of Faith from their dear German land,

"The Hermits of the Ridge," their life apart

From all that could allure the worldly heart,

Waiting the promised Virgin — she who fled

Into the forests, and should come, they said,

With the twelve stars a glory round her, soon,

Clothed with the sun, beneath her feet the moon,

And blessing all, and evermore to bless, —

The promised "Woman of the Wilderness!"

3

Ah, why delayed she? Still not purified

Were they to meet the coming of the Bride?

More prayer, more fasting, till the soul grew faint,

And weak the vision of the pure young saint;

And yet she came not — but she took to her,

Perhaps, the soul of her rapt worshipper;

And sitting near this spring, whose changeless stone

Remains to witness of the good man gone,

JOHN KELPIUS passed away from mortal sight,

And found at last the Virgin clothed in white.

Deep in the stream still lies the mystic stone,

The "stone of Wisdom," given to him alone,

Dropped by his hand, all faltering and slow,

In the clear wave, two hundred years ago.

"Who finds that stone of power, shall dream a dream!"

So runs the legend of the haunted stream.

Ah who would think amid this peaceful scene,

These solemn shades of hemlock, ever green,

These rugged rocks, with moss all cushioned o'er,

That once these hills had heard the cannon's roar?

That height had flung to height the heavy ball,

And echoed back the drum's defiant call,

While Armstrong's men responded with a cheer,

To the fierce shouts of Hessen's grenadier?

Gone are those days, and never to return!

The Past lies buried in its own sad urn.

Henceforth to us an Englishman shall be

But an American from o'er the sea,

Who speaks the language that a Shakspeare spoke,

And shares the spirit that in Hampden woke,

A countryman of PENN, and therefore more —

Our older brother from our father's shore.

Perish the hand that future strife would fire

Between these sons of one immortal sire;

And blest be he who binds their hearts in one,

In sacred links that ne'er shall be undone!

How changed our land since o'er these waters blue

The Indian warrior urged his light canoe;

Since o'er these hills the Lenni-Lennapee

Followed the flying deer with footstep free.

Thank God, no blood of his is on our hands!

Thank God, no blood of his pollutes our lands!

When first our fathers to his wigwam came,

He called us " brothers," and we owned the claim;

As o'er the earth one equal sky was spread,

So was one law for white man and for red.

And thus ev'n now, where'er the Indian brave,

From dark Missouri to Pacific's wave,

Flies to escape the inevitable doom,

Which takes a Continent, and gives a tomb,

He shrines the name of MIQUON in his breast,

As of the man, the wisest, truest, best;

Who, seeking good for one, sought good for both,

And whose plain word was better than an oath!

And now the white man treads these hills alone,

The "great, original people" * all are gone.

Build we ourselves then the grand COUNCIL FIRE,

And call each gallant son, each veteran sire.

Here where was born a Nation in a day,

A young Achilles, ready for the fray;

Here where so many memories gleam and glow

Of that long fight one hundred years ago,

---

* Lenni-Lennapee means "the original people" — which they claimed
to be. The great progenitors of the other tribes.

3 *

Here may all gather on this smooth, green sward,

And for his gracious mercies thank the Lord.

Here bring the fruits of earth, the spoils of art,

The boast of busy hands and wealthy mart,

Ripe brain of manhood, woman's kindly mouth,

Skill of the North, and richness of the South ;

And as we bring them, say with one accord,

"These are our First Fruits, great and blessed Lord !

Forgive us aught the Past has wrongly done,

And make the hearts of all the heart of one ;

Still bind our States in a well-ordered band,

Where Power shall walk with Freedom hand-in-hand ;

Where none shall claim a right he will not give,

Nor by his light force other men to live.

Thus bid all strife and sad contention cease,

By blessing all with Liberty and Peace !"

THE END.

CLAXTON, REMSEN & HAFFELFINGER,

PUBLISHERS, BOOKSELLERS AND STATIONERS,

624, 626 & 628 MARKET ST., PHILADELPHIA.

www.ingramcontent.com/pod-product-compliance
Lightning Source LLC
Chambersburg PA
CBHW030915260626
47169CB00008B/2856